SADDLEBACK *Classics*

T5-DHH-286

MOBY DICK

HERMAN MELVILLE

ADAPTED BY

Janet Lorimer

♡ For Nesta Riley ♡ Aug. 2010
Congrats. Son... on to 2nd grade...
We Love You.

SADDLEBACK PUBLISHING, INC.

SADDLEBACK *Classics*

The Adventures of Tom Sawyer
Dr. Jekyll and Mr. Hyde
Dracula
Great Expectations
Jane Eyre
Moby Dick
Robinson Crusoe
The Time Machine

Development and Production: Laurel Associates, Inc.
Cover and Interior Art: Black Eagle Productions

SADDLEBACK PUBLISHING, INC.
Three Watson,
Irvine, CA 92618-2767

ISBN 1-56254-258-3

Printed in the United States of America
09 08 07 06 05   9 8 7 6 5 4 3 2 1

CONTENTS

1 The Tattooed Harpooner

Call me Ishmael. Teaching school is my profession. But from time to time I feel a great need for more adventure. When that yearning comes over me, I leave my classroom and go to sea. There is something about the open seas that lifts up my spirits when I am feeling down.

I had never gone to sea as an officer or even as a cook, but as a common sailor. Some years ago I gained some experience in the merchant service. But this time I hungered for even more adventure: I wanted to become a whale hunter.

I knew there was good money in the trade. But that was not the only reason I wanted to go whaling. I must confess that I was interested in the whales themselves. They were such fascinating brutes. They seemed both mysterious and magnificent.

Once I made up my mind to go, I stuffed a couple of shirts into my knapsack. And although I had only a handful of coins in my pocket, I started off.

It was on a stormy Saturday night in December when I arrived in the coastal town of New Bedford. An icy wind chased me up and down the narrow streets as I searched for a place to stay. I shivered, as much from the silence as from the chill. The town seemed as cold and lonely as a tomb. My dark mood was no way to begin an adventure, but I could not shake myself free of it. Still, here I was. One way or another I had to find a room for the night.

The first lodging houses I passed seemed much too fancy and costly. I fingered the few coins in my pocket and hurried on down the street. At last I reached the docks. A strong smell of fish was in the air. I could hear the cold, dark water slapping the sides of ships and lapping at the wooden docks.

This was a poorer part of town. There were no street lamps to light my way.

Shivering again, I pulled my coat closer around me. Then ahead I saw a dim light in the window of an old building. The sign over the door read *The Spouter Inn—Peter Coffin, proprietor*. What a name for a landlord in this dark place! Still, I had nowhere else to go, and it looked as if I could afford to stay here.

The door was open, so I walked right in. Just beyond the entry hall was the common room. In the dim light I could make out a few tables and chairs. Across the room a weak fire burned in the fireplace, sending out more smoke than heat or light. On the wall over the fireplace hung a painting of a whale attacking a ship. Years of smoke from the fire had darkened the painting. But I could still make out the gigantic monster of the deep looming out of the water over the ship. I thought about my business in that town and shivered a little.

Another wall in the common room was decorated with a collection of whalers' tools. I saw harpoons, clubs, and spears. It wasn't a very cheerful room, but at least I was out of the cold and gloomy weather.

A few men sat about, talking and drinking. I found the landlord, Peter Coffin, and asked him for a room.

"Sorry, we're full up," he said. Then, as I started to turn away, he called me back. "Wait! You don't mind sharing a bed with a harpooner, do you?"

"I'd rather sleep alone," I said, "but if that's all you've got, I'll take it."

When the landlord asked if I wanted a meal, I was quick to answer yes. Before long, Mr. Coffin called out, "Grub, ho!" and all the men crowded around a long table in the dining room. Having no fireplace, this room was as cold as a North Atlantic iceberg. But when the food was served, we all found it good and hot.

After dinner, I asked the landlord if the harpooner had come in yet. Oddly enough, all the other men at the table stopped talking. They looked from me to the landlord with keen interest.

Peter Coffin grinned and shook his head. "No, he's not come in just yet. Perhaps he's having some trouble selling his head."

"His *what*?" I cried out. "Did you say he was trying to sell his head?"

"That's right," said the landlord. "I told him he couldn't sell it in New Bedford. The market here is overstocked."

"Now see here," I said firmly, "save your tall tales for someone else. I'm not a stupid, know-nothing greenhorn."

The landlord and the other sailors burst out laughing. This annoyed me even more, since I could not guess what was so funny. Finally Mr. Coffin took a breath. "Well," he said, "this harpooner just arrived from the South Seas. That's where he got the shrunken heads. He's sold all but one."

That did it! I decided I wouldn't wait up for the harpooner. I might have to share a bed with him, but I didn't want to talk to him. I climbed the stairs to the room we would share, undressed, and lay down on the wide bed.

At first I had a hard time falling asleep, but I must have dozed off. Then suddenly I heard footsteps outside the room. The door

banged open and an enormous man walked in! The flickering light of the bedside candle outlined his bulky form.

He was a giant of a man. And oh, what a face! He was not actually bad-looking, but his deeply tanned skin was tattooed all over with strange designs. When he took off his coat, I could see even more tattoos on his arms and chest. His head was bald except for a long black topknot.

Good heavens, I thought, was I sharing the bed with a cannibal? Drawing the covers over my head, I could hear the harpooner humming to himself as he got ready for bed.

He didn't seem to notice me. Had Peter Coffin forgotten to tell him that I was there? I felt the bed sag a little as he crawled under the covers. Then, in the next moment, the tattooed man looked in my face, yanked the covers off, and let out a terrible cry.

§2 Signing on the *Pequod*

The startled harpooner jumped back in alarm. He looked as frightened as I was! "Who you be?" he shouted.

Before I could answer, he seized his tomahawk and raised it over his head.. He shook the tomahawk as if he meant to bash in my skull. "*Who you be?*" he demanded again in his broken English.

I sat up against the head of the bed and called out, "Landlord! Please save me!"

Awakened by the shouts, Peter Coffin quickly came running in. "What's all the noise about?" he hissed. "Everyone's trying to sleep!" Then he saw the problem and burst out laughing. "Queequeg, put the tomahawk down, man. This is Ishmael. He means you no harm."

The landlord then properly introduced me

to the huge harpooner. He explained that Queequeg was a native of an island in the South Seas. He might *look* fierce, but he was really a gentle soul.

Giving me a big grin, Queequeg slapped me hard on the shoulder. He meant it as a friendly gesture, but he almost knocked me out of bed. Then he dropped his tomahawk on the floor and climbed in beside me.

"Better to sleep with a sober cannibal," I thought, "than with a drunken Christian." So we both closed our eyes and fell asleep. I have never slept better in all my life.

The next day Queequeg and I began to get to know each other. Before the day was over we were fast friends. Queequeg, I learned, was the son of a tribal chief. His tribe were a seafaring people who lived in a faraway land called Aotearoa, which meant "the long white cloud."

Queequeg told me that he had left his homeland to see the world. When a ship docked at the island, he tried to go aboard. But the captain said there was no room for him. Later that night he swam out to the ship and hid on board. By the time the crew found him, it was too late to turn back.

The ship's captain had taught Queequeg how to harpoon whales. "I sail around whole world on that ship," Queequeg said with pride. "I see many strange places and strange people. I learn many new things."

When I told him about my wish for a whaling adventure, we agreed to ship out together. Queequeg carried his own harpoon, a huge weapon with a handle made of whale bone.

Not only did he use the harpoon to kill whales, I discovered that Queequeg also shaved with it! Later, when we went downstairs for breakfast, Queequeg used his harpoon at the table to spear pieces of meat. He had very good aim. I noticed that no man got in Queequeg's way nor made fun of this gentle giant.

Because it was a Sunday morning, there was little to do. I wanted to walk about and look the town over. Queequeg and I found we were not alone. The town was quite crowded with other men who had come from every part of the country to seek their fortunes at sea.

Then the icy wind picked up and the weather went bad. We were looking for shelter when we came upon a small chapel and slipped inside. The service was about to begin, so we quickly found seats in one of the pews. At least it was warmer in the church than it was outdoors!

The organist was playing a hymn. The old organ tended to squeak at the high notes and wheeze at the low notes. But the members of the congregation were singing right along. As I joined in, I glanced about me. The walls of the chapel were decorated with plaques bearing the names of sailors killed at sea. I also noticed that many of the women in the church were dressed in black. They must be the widows of the dead whalers! Again I began to worry about the dangers of whale hunting, but I decided that it was too late to turn back.

A retired harpooner named Father Mapple gave the sermon. His pulpit was built to look like the prow of a ship. Today his sermon was about Jonah and the whale. It was a good subject for a bunch of men who were soon to ship out to sea.

The next day Queequeg and I sailed to Nantucket, an island off the coast of Massachusetts. Nantucket was a sandy, barren place. But I had heard it was a fine seaport, famous as a base for whale hunters. I was sure we would find a whaling ship to hire us there.

There were three whaling ships in port. We looked them over very carefully. At last we settled on one called the *Pequod*. For some reason we liked the look of her. She was a big, old-fashioned ship, well-seasoned and weather-stained.

One of the owners, a crusty old sailor named Peleg, was on deck. He was signing on a new crew. I explained that I wanted to sign on. I said I wanted to see the world and find out what whaling was all about.

"Oh, so you want to see what whaling is all about, do you?" the old man said. He cracked a grin. "Have you seen our Captain Ahab yet?"

I shook my head. "And who is Captain Ahab?" I asked politely.

"Why, the captain of this ship," said Peleg. "The man you'll take your orders from."

"Well," I said, "I should very much like to meet him. Where is he?"

Peleg gave me a strange smile. "He does not wish to see anyone right now," said the old man. "The captain is not, uh—feeling well. But never fear. He will be well enough when it's time to sail."

"I'm sorry to hear that he's under the weather," I said. Somehow I sensed that Peleg was trying to tell me something strange about the captain. But I couldn't for the life of me figure out what it was.

"He has only one leg," Peleg went on. "The other one was bit off by a whale." He peered at me as if wondering how I would respond. When I said nothing, he added, "No matter what you may think, your captain is not as evil as King Ahab in the Bible. Do you still want to sign on?"

I nodded. I don't know if he was trying to make me feel better or trying to scare me off. But if he thought I might change my mind, he would have to think again.

"I have a friend who wants to sign on, too," I added.

"Bring him along," said the old man. But when he saw Queequeg, he began to have second thoughts. "I'm not sure I want a wild-looking pagan covered with tattoos on my ship," he said suspiciously. "Can he harpoon whales?"

"Why, he's killed more whales than you can count!" I said. "Queequeg, show him your skill."

Queequeg motioned us to follow him to the side of the ship. He pointed to a small dot of tar floating in the water. "You see spot of tar? Suppose that be whale's eye." He lifted his great harpoon and threw it. The sharp point went right into the spot of tar— like an arrow into a bullseye!

As Queequeg reeled in his harpoon, the ship owner's eyes opened wide. "Quick!" he said to me. "I must have that harpooner on my ship." Then he turned to Queequeg. "You! Quohog, can you write your name?"

"His name is Queequeg," I said sharply.

"Peequeg, Quohog, whatever he wants to be called," Captain Peleg said. He thrust a pen at Queequeg. My friend could not read or write English, but he carefully made an X where his name was supposed to go. When I signed my name right under his, we turned to each other and smiled. My adventure was about to begin!

3

We Meet the Crew

The next few days were busy ones aboard the *Pequod*. What a big job it was to make the ship ready for her voyage! There were sails to mend and rigging to repair. There was food to store—beef, bread, and water—as well as other supplies—tools, iron nails, canvas, and rope. The *Pequod* would be at sea for three long years. We would have to carry everything we might need for all those long months.

At last the day came when we were to sail. It dawned cold and gray. Queequeg and I had been staying at a nearby inn while the ship was being made ready. Now we arose early and packed our gear.

After breakfast we set out for the docks. The gray fog wrapped itself around us like a wet muffler. We could see no more than a few feet in any direction. I could hear ships' bells clanging, sailors laughing and talking, and the sound of water splashing against the pilings. But all these sounds were muffled.

As we neared the ship, Queequeg and I saw several shadowy figures hurrying up the gangplank. But before we could join them, I felt a heavy hand clasp my shoulder. I turned, startled, and found myself face-to-face with an odd-looking old fellow.

He was dressed in the patched and ragged clothes of a sailor. His face was badly scarred. What startled me so was the strange glow in his eyes. "Going aboard?" he asked in a voice that cracked like a broken timber.

"Take your hand off," I demanded, shoving him away. "Who are you?"

"Name's Elijah," said the stranger. He leaned forward, peering into my face. "Tell me, have you signed on the *Pequod*?" he asked with a strange glint in his eye.

"Yes, we've signed on. And you?"

He lowered his voice, glancing left and right. "Have you seen Old Thunder yet— Captain Ahab himself?"

"No, not yet," I said. "We were told he was not well—but we expect to see him soon. Why do you ask, old man?"

Elijah let out a horrible chuckle. He raised his other arm and I saw that his hand was gone. He shook the stump at us. "The day old Ahab is well is the day this arm is made whole!" he cackled.

I didn't like the way the man was acting nor what he said. I motioned to Queequeg that we should move on. "This fellow is not right in the head," I muttered.

"But if you've already signed on, then it's too late. What's done is done," Elijah stopped suddenly. "Good morning to you." He started to hobble away.

"Too late for *what*?" I called after him.

"I won't be seeing you again," he called back. "Sailing on a doomed ship, you are. Heaven help you, mates. Heaven help you." He disappeared into the fog.

As we walked up the gangplank, I noticed how quiet the ship was. It was as if Queequeg and I were the only two people on board. I remembered the ghostly figures

I'd seen hurrying up the gangplank. Where were they now? Then I thought of Elijah's warning. I tried to tell myself that the silence and the fog were getting on my nerves. But in spite of my excitement, I could not shake an uneasy feeling about this voyage.

Queequeg and I went below to claim our bunks and stow our gear. No one was below deck either. So we sat back to wait for further orders, and before long we heard noises on deck. The rest of the crew and the last of the supplies were coming on board. At last the ship was nearly ready to sail. Where was Captain Ahab, and when would we meet him?

The *Pequod* set sail on Christmas day. We moved off into the cold, gray Atlantic, not knowing what adventures awaited us.

Over the next few days Queequeg and I met the other members of the crew. They had come from every corner of the world. Like all groups of men, they were good and bad and all things in between. But all of us had one thing in common—a love of the sea and a desire to hunt whales.

The first mate was a fine-looking fellow named Starbuck. He was a tall, sturdy man, who seemed to have an even temper and a kind nature. In time I learned that Starbuck had lost both a father and a brother to the sea. But these losses had not made him bitter. Killing whales was no less and no more than a job to him.

A jolly fellow named Stubb was the second mate. He didn't seem to take much seriously. We often heard him singing to himself as he went about his work. And he liked to crack jokes with other members of the crew.

Flask, the third mate, was a man who lived to kill whales. He made it clear that he hated all whales, and he was sure that they hated him.

The harpooners were next in importance. They had to be very brave, very strong men, with clear eyes and powerful arms. Besides Queequeg, the other two harpooners were an American Indian named Tashtego and an African named Daggoo. Tashtego was a member of a strong, fearless New England tribe that hunted whales. Daggoo's people were the brave warriors of an African tribe. He had gained his skill with a harpoon by throwing spears as a lion hunter.

As for those ghostly figures I'd seen the day we came aboard, they were a special crew of oarsmen. Ahab had handpicked each one of them. They would row Captain Ahab's own boat when a whale was sighted.

The crew leader was an Arab named Fedallah. He was Ahab's own harpooner. It was said that he could tell fortunes and see into the future. I wondered what kind of fortune he saw for this crew. Then I decided I didn't want to know! I also wondered why Ahab would hire a special crew. Were we not hunting ordinary whales?

We still had not seen the mysterious Captain. But we heard stories about him from other sailors who'd sailed with him in the past. Some said that Ahab had a kind of evil inside him that had poisoned him and constantly made him suffer. Some said that the evil in Ahab was a kind of power passed to him from the whale that had bitten off his leg.

I thought all the stories sounded like tall tales, but at the same time I could not shake my uneasy feelings. How long would it be before the captain appeared to take command of his ship? What kind of captain would he be?

I did not have too long to wait.

4 Captain Ahab's Mission

Heading directly south, the *Pequod* finally entered warmer waters. I was glad to leave the North Atlantic behind, with its cold, gray skies and mountains of white ice floating in a cold, gray sea.

The southern waters were a beautiful blue color that matched the blue sky overhead. Everything I saw in this part of the world was new and exciting. Sometimes we sailed near islands, their green mountains crowned with white clouds. Sometimes we passed schools of porpoises playing in the sea.

Then one day, while I was scouring the deck, a shadow fell across me. I looked up and there at last stood Captain Ahab on the quarterdeck. The man was dressed from head to toe in black. I gasped. Perhaps his face had once been good and kind, but now it had such evil in it as I have never seen before and hope never to see again!

A long white scar sliced his weather-beaten face from his forehead down to his neck. It reminded me of the ugly scar that a bolt of lightning sometimes burns into a tree trunk. I wondered if the same whale that had bitten off his leg had also scarred Ahab's face. The captain's dark hair was peppered with gray and blew wildly in the wind. Ahab had strapped a peg leg made of whale ivory to the stump of his thigh. I saw that he anchored the peg leg into a hole in the deck to help him keep his balance.

It was his eyes that made me shudder. They were filled with a dark fire that could not have been natural. His gaze was fierce and fearless. Whatever drove this man, I thought, was indeed a powerful evil. I remembered Elijah's warning: "Heaven help you, mates. *Heaven help you!*"

Suddenly Ahab called out to the crew. "You men on top of the mastheads—look sharp now! There are whales in these waters. If you see a white whale, shout the signal at once!"

A *white* whale, I thought to myself—now that would be a strange sight. Before I could wonder more about that white whale, Ahab ordered Starbuck to gather the crew together.

Starbuck seemed worried. "Is something wrong, sir?" I understood his concern. That order was given only in an emergency.

"Don't ask questions," Ahab growled. "Do as you're told. And bring me a hammer and nail while you're at it."

When we were all gathered together on deck, Ahab asked what we would do if we spotted a whale. To a man, the whole crew cried out the answer. "Call the signal, Captain: *There she blows!*"

Ahab nodded, a grim smile twisting his lips. "Yes! And what do you do next?"

"Lower the whale boats, sir," we answered. "We go after the whale. Kill it. Then we tow the body back to the ship, strip the blubber, and melt it down."

Ahab nodded, smiling. He seemed pleased with our answers. Why, I wondered, would he ask such simple questions? Most of this crew were seasoned sailors.

Then Ahab reached into his pocket and pulled out a shiny gold coin. He held it up for every man to see. We gazed at the gold in silence.

"You've heard talk of a white whale," Ahab said. He took the hammer and nailed the gold coin to the mast. "You see this gold coin?" he went on. "It's a Spanish gold ounce worth 16 dollars!"

The crew gasped. That was a splendid amount of money for any man!

"The first man who spots the white whale will have this coin," Ahab roared. Daggoo stepped forward, his forehead knotted with worry. "Captain, is that white whale the one they call Moby Dick?"

"Aye," said the Captain excitedly. "The beast I seek has a wrinkled brow and a crooked jaw."

"With many harpoons twisted into his hump?" yelled Tashtego.

Ahab nodded, his eyes glowing. "*Yes!* Rusted in him like old corkscrews—and some of those harpoons are mine!"

"Was that the whale that took your leg, Captain?" asked Starbuck.

Ahab turned on his first mate. His eyes were wild and wicked looking. "Who told you that?" he bellowed. Then, before Starbuck could answer, he almost sobbed. "It's true. It's the white monster that took my leg—but *I'll have him* this time! I'll chase him from here to Norway if I have to. Nay, I'll chase him across all the seven seas until he spouts black blood and is gone forever!" Then Ahab took a ragged breath and gazed at the men around him. "So what say you, mates? Will you help me give chase to that cursed whale?"

"Aye, Captain. Aye! Aye!" the men all shouted. All but one, that is.

As the crew cheered, Starbuck stood alone and silent, a look of horror and disgust on his face.

Ahab saw the look and glared at the first mate. "Well, Starbuck? Are you not brave enough to give chase to the white whale?"

"Courage has nothing to do with it," muttered Starbuck. "It is madness to be so angry at a dumb animal. The white whale did not strike you out of hatred, but out of fear. I came to hunt whales for their oil, Captain, not to get revenge."

Ahab's lip curled in a sneer. He ordered us to get back to work and paid no further attention to Starbuck's grumbling. We knew that we had work to do. Our job was to kill as many whales as we could, strip off the blubber, and melt it down into oil. The more barrels we filled, the more money we'd be paid at the end of the voyage.

In the days that followed, we sailed through good weather and bad. Some days the sea was so peaceful the ship rocked as gently as a baby's cradle. Other days, storms ripped at the masts and tore at the rigging.

Always, the lookout stood high on the mast to watch for whales. It was a dangerous place to be. First, he had to climb the rigging. If he put a foot wrong or missed a handhold, he could easily fall to his death.

The first time Starbuck ordered me to the lookout, I began my climb willingly. But halfway to the top, I made the mistake of looking down. The deck seemed a mile below me, and the sailors looked like tiny mice scurrying about.

My head began to whirl, and I felt dizzy. Shutting my eyes, I held tightly to the ropes. Everything swayed—the ship, the mast, and the rigging. I swallowed hard and took a deep breath. Then I opened my eyes and looked up until the dizziness passed. I did not look down again until I reached the lookout.

"There She Blows!"

"There she blows!" I was mending a sail one day when I heard the lookout give the cry! "Three points to starboard, mates."

Jumping to my feet, I ran to the starboard side of the ship. In the distance I could see a towering fountain of water jutting out of the sea. It was blowing out of a hole on top of the whale's head!

Starbuck was excited. "Quick, men," he shouted. "Lower the boats!"

Queequeg and I jumped into Starbuck's boat, I as an oarsman and Queequeg as the harpooner. Starbuck stood in the prow, urging us to row harder toward the whale. We rowed as fast as we could, chasing the black monster through the slick green waves. Then all at once, we felt a chill wind blast into our faces. Looking up, we saw the sky rapidly darkening with inky clouds.

"Row, mates, row! Put your backs into it, lads," Starbuck roared. "There's a storm coming, but we've got time to kill a whale."

We pulled in as close as we dared. In high excitement, I found myself staring at a sperm whale! Of all the whales in the sea, the sperm whale was the biggest. It also produced the most valuable kind of oil. This one was perhaps 90 feet long. Its head alone made up about a third of the creature. The rest of its body looked much like that of a fish, although it did not have scales and gills.

The whale has an eye on each side of its head. I was surprised to see that they were not very large. Nor were its ears big either, being nothing but small holes just behind the eyes. The whale's mouth is another story. The jaws are about 15 feet long. Spike-like teeth line both top and bottom jaws.

Starbuck told us to ship the oars, meaning to pull them from the water. We did so, floating next to the great black hump that rose out of the water.

"*There*, Queequeg," Starbuck whispered.

"Throw your harpoon, man!"

Queequeg rose up in the pitching boat. Standing with his legs wide to hold his balance, he raised the great harpoon. But just at that moment, the storm hit us with full fury. Lightning flashed, thunder rolled, and the skies opened up, lashing us with a freezing rain. As Queequeg threw the harpoon, the great beast dove beneath the waves and escaped.

By now, all about us was cloaked in darkness. Because we could not see the *Pequod*, we huddled in our boat, wet, cold and growing hungry. For hours the rain poured down and wind drove the cold right through our clothes, all the way to the bone. Waiting for a break in the weather, we floated all night in our waterlogged boat.

Then suddenly, just before dawn, Queequeg jumped to his feet. He turned this way and that as if listening for something.

"What is it?" I asked. Then we all heard the frightening sounds of wood splintering and rope creaking.

"Look out, men," Starbuck yelled out to

us. "*Jump! Save yourselves!*"

I dove overboard with the others—and not a moment too soon! Just as I hit the water I heard a terrible crunching sound. The *Pequod* had hit our whale boat. In the darkness, the crew had not seen us—but they soon heard our cries.

We were quickly pulled from the ocean. How grateful we all were for warm, dry clothes and a hot meal! Later, I had a word with Starbuck about our near miss.

"Does this kind of thing happen often?" I asked. "We lost the whale and then were nearly killed by our own ship!"

"Aye, lad," the first mate said with a sad smile. "Whaling is a dangerous business. The dark angel of death is always with us."

I was disappointed that we had lost the whale, but the next bit of excitement was soon to come. A giant squid! It was the following day when the lookout spotted the creature. We all ran to the side of the ship to look at this odd beast.

Even now I hardly know how to describe it. It looked as if it were all head and arms.

I saw that the arms were lined with suckers. One of the sailors told me that squid could hold on to things with those suckers. He said they had seen the marks of suckers on whales. It boggled my mind. I tried to imagine a whale and a giant squid in battle.

Two of the creature's ten arms were much longer than the other eight. One of the sailors said that a squid used those arms to grab its prey. Then it would chew the victim with its sharp mouth. The thought made me shudder. The tentacled beast had eyes that looked almost human.

No doubt about it—that squid was the most fearful-looking creature I had ever seen. But some of the sailors were glad to see it. "Where there are squid, there are whales," they said.

Not long after that, the lookout spotted a school of whales—hundreds of them! Again the cry went up. "There she blows! There she blows!"

Again, the boats were lowered and we were after the whales. As our oars cut through the tossing waves, I realized how

small and helpless we were in this vast, watery world. All around us the monstrous black backs of the whales broke the surface. Now harpoon after harpoon was hurled at the huge humps, the sharp points cutting through the whales' flesh.

Any harpoon is like a giant spear. But some have handles made of wood. Others, like Queequeg's, had ivory handles. At the end of a harpoon is a knifelike metal tip. It is always kept very sharp so it can pierce both the whale's tough skin and the thick layer of valuable blubber right below it.

The length of rope that is tied to the harpoon is also tied to the boat. When a harpoon slices into the whale's body, the whale tries to escape. But no matter how far it swims, the whale is bound to the whale boat by that rope. The real danger to sailors is if the whale dives deeply enough to carry the boat with it! Then there is nothing to do but cut the rope and set the whale free.

The school of whales we were hunting tried to get away, but there were too many of them. They got in each other's way. Although their great, strong tails beat the water into foam, the water gushing from their blowholes blew red with blood. Soon blood stained the green water all around us as thick clots came welling up out of the whales' wounds. Then, one by one, the tails and flukes went limp and the animals stopped moving as they died.

We towed the huge carcasses back to the *Pequod*. Once on board, we went to work, cutting blubber from the mammoth bodies. Then the blubber was chopped into chunks and thrown into huge pots that hung over big fires. When the fire melted the fat, we stored the whale oil in barrels.

Finally, the rest of the carcass was cut loose for the sharks and other fish to feed on. As I watched the butchered carcasses float away, I felt a little sad. It seemed a sorry end for such splendid animals!

6 Searching for Moby Dick

The *Pequod*'s voyage continued. Days turned into weeks, and weeks became months. Now and then we passed other whaling ships. Usually, a whaling ship carries mail for other ships it might meet along the way. The letters were months old, of course, but the men were lonely and any news was welcome. Once, however, we tried to deliver a letter to a man who had recently been killed in a whaling accident.

Our meetings with other ships should have been pleasant times for our crew. Most captains were glad for a chance to let their men catch up on news. Not Captain Ahab! Each time we came upon a ship, Ahab would hail it with the single question, "Have you seen a white whale?"

Most often the answer was no, but once

in a while it was a loud "Aye!"

When he heard that word Ahab's eyes would take on a gleam. "*Where?*" he would demand. "How long ago? Is the whale still alive or did you kill it?"

Our Captain could be quite rude if he did not get the answers he wanted. Once he found out what he wanted to know, he would immediately order Starbuck to sail off in the direction of the white whale.

One day Starbuck discovered that a few of the oil barrels were leaking in the hold. He told Ahab that there was an island some miles away. We could find wood there to mend the barrels. There was only one small problem: Sailing to the island would take us off course for a few days.

"No!" Ahab snapped. He was on deck with his chart spread out in front of him. The chart showed where different types of whales swam, and the Captain was using it to track Moby Dick.

Starbuck gritted his teeth. "Captain Ahab, that oil is our bread and butter, so to speak," Starbuck argued. "The men have worked long and hard, and taken great risks to get it. Now you put them at risk of losing the money they have earned."

For a moment, Ahab was silent. We could all see that he was trying to control his anger. Then he nodded. "We'll do as you say, Starbuck," Ahab growled. "Turn the ship. Let us get the wood."

After we had cut the wood and brought it on board, we returned to our search for Moby Dick. Meantime, we had to fix the barrels. That meant that someone had to go down into the hold. No one wanted to go there. The place was cold and wet and had a horrible smell. At last Queequeg agreed to go down. My friend found the barrels that were leaking and repaired them.

Unfortunately, he also caught a chill. Before long the chill turned to fever. Nothing seemed to help Queequeg. He lay in his bunk, tossing and turning. He would not eat and could take only a few sips of water. I watched helplessly as he grew thinner and thinner. It was as if his life force were burning out of him. I feared that my friend Queequeg was going to die.

"Queequeg, you *must* eat," I told him. "You must gain back your strength. Please eat something—I beg you." I held out a bowl of hot broth for him to sip, but he turned his head aside.

"Get carpenter," he muttered hoarsely. "I must talk to carpenter."

"No," I said crossly. Why wouldn't this stubborn man try to help himself? "First, you must eat."

"Leave him be," Starbuck said gently. "I've seen cases like this before. Do as he says—get the carpenter."

With a sinking heart, I fetched the ship's carpenter. Queequeg asked the carpenter to build him a wooden coffin shaped like a canoe. "Make coffin tight," he told the carpenter. "No water get into canoe."

When the carpenter agreed, Queequeg lay back in his bunk and closed his eyes. I dreaded the day the last nail would go into that coffin. It seemed certain that the last day of my friend's life was drawing near.

Then a strange thing happened! The very

day the coffin was finished, Queequeg's
chills and fever suddenly disappeared. He
sat up in his bunk and asked for food. I was
delighted to see that his eyes were clear and
his voice was strong again.

"Tell me, my friend. What will you do
with your coffin now?" I asked.

Queequeg smiled. "Coffin make fine sea
chest," he said. He packed some of his gear
into the coffin and nailed it shut.

Our ship was getting close to the waters
near Japan. That was where Ahab's enemy

Moby Dick had last been seen.

Then for some strange reason, the rolling seas became calm! *Too* calm, in fact. For days, no breath of wind moved the sails. At dawn, the sun would rise in the east and slowly make its way across the sky. There it burned overhead like a great white lamp. We had no relief from its hot light. In the sun's rays, the gold coin that Ahab had nailed to the mast gleamed like an evil eye.

The crew didn't like it. We tried to find what little shade we could, and we drank our supply of water sparingly. We all knew what would happen if we ran out of fresh water. If a man tried to live on salt water, he would go mad and die.

The terrible heat made it hard to sleep. Our bunks were like steam rooms. Up on deck, the sun beat down without mercy. Not a one of us was getting much rest.

One morning a tired sailor, climbing to the lookout post, lost his footing. We heard his terrified scream as he fell from the rigging and the terrible silence after he plunged into the water.

47

"Man overboard!" shouted Daggoo, as he threw a life preserver into the sea.

We lowered a boat while we watched for the sailor to bob up to the surface. But he did not. Oddly enough, the life preserver Daggoo had thrown to him sank also.

Everyone was getting more and more nervous. The sailor's death seemed like a bad omen. Had we been cursed with bad luck? Even Captain Ahab seemed to feel it. He told Fedallah about a bad dream he'd had. "I saw a big hearse come to carry me away," the Captain said.

Fedallah pulled a small bag from his pocket. He poured out a handful of strange little stones with odd marks on them. Kneeling down, he shook the little stones about, and tossed them onto the deck. Then he studied the stones carefully. "No, you will not have a hearse, Captain—nor even a coffin when you die."

Ahab's eyes grew wide. "Does this mean I will die at sea?" he asked.

Fedallah leaned close to Ahab. "Before you die, you will see *two* hearses. The first one will not be made by human hands. The second one will be made of wood that grows in America." Fedallah paused, eyeing Ahab. "*I* will die before you, my captain—so that I may pilot you to the next world."

"What are you saying, man?" Ahab hissed. "Will I kill Moby Dick or won't I? Will I live or will I die?"

Fedallah gazed at Ahab. Then he said, "It will be a rope that kills you."

7

Starbuck Challenges Ahab

The Captain was quiet for a long while after Fedallah told him how he would die. Then Ahab turned to gaze into the distance. "Forty years," he muttered. "Forty years of my life given to the sea." For a moment, tears of loneliness—or was it regret?—seemed to douse the evil light in his eye.

Seeing Ahab's face go soft, Starbuck came forward. "Captain, please! Let's go home now! We have enough oil. We all miss our families. Give up this mad dream of killing the white whale."

Ahab immediately drew back in fury. "Give up? *Never!* Not until the black heart of that white whale has stopped beating."

I sometimes look back on that day even now. I wonder if things might have been different if Ahab had not said what he did. I remembered that Fedallah hadn't said whether or not Ahab would kill Moby Dick. And he had said nothing about the rest of our voyage. But I think his remarks to Ahab left us all with a sense of doom.

We saw a change in Starbuck. He had grown even angrier with the Captain. We had more than enough oil in the barrels. The owners would be pleased with their profit.

At the same time, we all knew that Ahab's search for Moby Dick had nothing to do with pleasing the owners. It didn't matter how many barrels we had filled nor how much money the oil would bring. The trouble was, our lives were in Ahab's hands.

Late one night, I found myself unable to sleep. Hoping to find a breath of cool air, I decided to go on deck. Beneath the full moon, I moved to the prow of the ship to gaze out on the glistening water.

Then suddenly, on the other side of the Captain's cabin, I heard Ahab arguing with the first mate. They must have thought themselves alone, because both of their voices were raised in anger.

I heard Starbuck beg the Captain to give up his foolish search for the white whale, and then I heard the Captain mock Starbuck's courage. Starbuck replied, quite patiently I thought, but there was a dangerous edge to his voice. I wondered how much longer he could remain calm.

Worried now, I moved forward quietly, hugging the shadows. As I edged toward them, I saw the Captain turn his back on the first mate. "You may think whatever you like about me, Starbuck. But I am still the Captain. And as long as I am, *I* will give the orders and you will obey. Do you understand?"

Starbuck's lips drew back over his teeth in fury. Then I saw the first mate reach into his coat and pull out a small pistol. Moonlight glinted off the barrel.

I held my breath and my heart pounded. Surely Starbuck would not go so far as to murder the Captain! Such madness could only bring about more madness. To kill the Captain would be as mad an act as Ahab's

crazed search for the white whale.

Starbuck seemed to pull himself together. He stared at the gun for a moment, and then his shoulders seemed to droop. Just as Ahab turned to face him, he tucked the gun back into his coat pocket.

To this day I do not know if Ahab guessed what Starbuck had nearly done. If so, he showed nothing of his feelings. All the Captain said was, "Well, Starbuck, do you understand? I am the Captain and I will be obeyed. Is that clear?"

"Aye, Captain," Starbuck said bitterly.

He was about to go below decks, when Ahab put his hand on his arm. "I'm not afraid of you, Starbuck," he said sharply.

A sour smile twisted Starbuck's mouth. "You have nothing to fear from me, old man. *Ahab should fear Ahab*," he said, before he strode away into the dark.

In silence, Ahab watched him go. I saw that the Captain had a thoughtful look on his face as he entered his cabin. As for me, I decided to return to my bunk. I hoped that I could now find sleep and that my dreams would not be nightmares.

The next day our calm weather turned bad. At first there was just a band of clouds on the horizon, but the storm blew in fast. It was the worst kind of storm—a typhoon!

As the rain poured down, our ship pitched back and forth in the rough waves. Lightning flashed overhead and thunder rolled. All hands were on deck, shifting the sails and desperately trying to keep the *Pequod* from capsizing.

We fought the storm for hours. I don't

think there was a sailor among us who was not worn out. But finally the storm seemed to weaken. The winds and waves became less angry.

All at once one of the sailors cried out. "Look! Look there—the masts!"

We looked toward where he was pointing. An eerie light flickered in the rigging and over the sails. It was as if the masts were on fire—but what strange flames they were! This fire burned with a cold glow that flashed both green and white. I had never seen anything like it before, but some of the other sailors had.

"Saint Elmo's Fire!" Stubb cried out. "Have mercy on us. It must be a sign."

"Who is Saint Elmo?" I exclaimed to the third mate.

Flask seemed surprised at the question. "Why, he's the patron saint of sailors, lad. Aye, this be a sign—but good or bad I cannot say."

Ahab was delighted with the eerie blaze. Dancing in the sky, it lit up the whole ship. His eyes mirrored the strange green and white flames. "Aye, men, look upon the fire!" he bellowed into the wind. "It lights the way to the white whale, Moby Dick."

"Or to our death," Tashtego muttered. Those who heard him nodded, and quickly stepped away from Ahab. It was as if they thought his madness for the whale were a sickness they might catch.

Seeing their retreat, Ahab lunged for the chest that held the harpoons and flung open the lid. Seizing a harpoon, he lifted it over his head so that it touched the mast.

The weird fire raced down the mast and jumped onto the metal tip of the harpoon. I had never before seen fire burn metal! Now I shuddered at the sight, wondering what strange power had created it.

The sailors drew back in horror. *"Evil!"* cried one. "The Captain is in league with—"

Starbuck grasped Ahab's shoulder. "Captain, *we must go back*. This ship is doomed. The voyage is doomed! For the sake of God, let us turn back for home."

Ahab pushed Starbuck away. Then he turned to the crew and lifted the glowing harpoon over his head. "Remember, men!

All of you promised to hunt the white whale. But for those of you who are afraid—" He ran his fingers down the metal, then blew on the harpoon and put out the flames. "—I blow out the last of our fears!"

The men were quite shocked by what Ahab had done. As the crew talked later, I could tell that we were divided in our thoughts. Some believed that Ahab had control of the evil force that pushed him after Moby Dick. But others believed that the evil power was in control of the Captain.

I myself did not know what to think, but I was very uneasy.

8 The *Rachel* Seeks Help

By the next afternoon the storm had passed. The black clouds had shredded into ragged pieces that were now floating in an orange sky. The sea mirrored the warm glow of the sun as it sank toward the horizon. It seemed that the whole world was bathed in a warm light. If this were a sign, perhaps it was a good one! I began to think that we might be all right after all.

A few days later, we came upon another whaling ship, the *Rachel*. As our ships drew alongside each other, Ahab hailed the *Rachel*'s captain. "Ahoy, Captain Gardiner! Have you seen a white whale?"

"Aye, we saw the whale yesterday," called Captain Gardiner. "We lowered our boats and went after the beast—but it turned and attacked us. Has your crew seen one of our whale boats drifting about?"

Ahab waved the captain's question aside. "Where was the white whale?" he cried out. "Did you kill him?"

Captain Gardiner looked angry. "You don't seem to understand, Ahab. The white whale was too much for us. Now one of my boats is lost and my own *son* is on it. The boy is still a child, only 12 years old. Captain Ahab, please—I beg you—for the love of God, *help me find my son!*"

We were all touched by the pain and sorrow in Captain Gardiner's voice. But Ahab only ground his teeth with impatience. "No, we haven't the time. I must go after the whale," Ahab cried out.

We were all stunned at how coldhearted Ahab was in the face of the man's grief.

"You cannot mean it, Captain Ahab," Mr. Stubb said. "Why, it's Captain Gardiner's son—his *boy*! We must try to save him. Tell Captain Gardiner we'll be glad to help."

"I will not!" Ahab roared. "Forgive me, Captain Gardiner, but I cannot do it. I must go after Moby Dick. He's close by now—I

can feel it in my bones. And I'm losing time by talking to you."

Captain Gardiner and his crew were as surprised as we were by Ahab's lack of sympathy. It wasn't natural. But what could any of us do? Ahab was the captain. When he told us to sail on, we had to obey.

From that moment on, Ahab stayed on deck. He ate on deck and he slept standing up. He had himself lifted into the rigging so he could keep a constant lookout for the white whale. And all the while, Ahab's harpooner Fedallah stood by, patiently and silently waiting.

Days went by. We saw nothing. Then one day Ahab called out to us from the lookout's post. "There she blows off the lee side! Look at that white hump, like an island of snow in the middle of the ocean. *It is Moby Dick!*"

We all rushed to gaze at the whale we'd been chasing around the world! Sure enough, I could clearly see the whale's white hump. A fountain of silver water was spouting from its blow hole. Ahab had been right about one thing: Moby Dick was a *monster* of a whale. The creature had to be twice the size of any of the whales we'd seen so far.

"Ha!" yelled Ahab. He lowered himself out of the rigging and limped to the mast where the gold coin was nailed. "I saw the whale first, lads. The gold is mine!"

He yanked the coin from the mast and stuffed it into his pocket. I think we all felt a bit disappointed. Each of us had secretly hoped to be the first one to spot the whale.

Ahab grinned at our unhappy faces. "Did

you not smell the whale?" he called out to us. "Did you not smell that odor of seaweed and barnacles and fish? That's the way Moby Dick smells—like an island. And look, do you see the birds?"

Sure enough, a flock of sea birds circled over that white hump. "The birds follow the beast," Ahab said. "Just watch for the birds, lads—they'll show you where the white whale is."

He signaled for the whale boats to be lowered. Before climbing into one of them, Ahab saw Starbuck standing near the wheel. The first mate's arms were crossed over his chest and his chin was stubbornly thrust out.

"Avast, Starbuck," Ahab growled. "Will you not come with us to hunt the whale? I thought you wanted the men to have more money. Well, do as you wish. This monster whale alone will bring enough oil to make us all rich."

"We have enough oil now, Captain," Starbuck snarled. "I will not hunt down this whale with you. The white whale is not the monster. The monster is inside *you*! You hunt it only for the sake of revenge."

Ahab's lips curled in anger. "Then stay here on the *Pequod*," he snapped, as he eased himself into the small boat. Not once did he look back at Starbuck. In a moment all the boats had shoved off, leaving only Starbuck and a handful of sailors to man the big ship.

As we rowed toward the whale, Moby Dick suddenly dove beneath the waves. A heavy silence then surrounded us. At the Captain's order, we shipped oars—waiting, watching, straining to hear. Overhead the birds circled. Their cries sounded oddly like the mewing of a cat.

For a few moments I closed my eyes and listened. I heard the birds cry, the soft slap of water against the boat, and the creak of our wooden craft rocking in the waves. The air felt cool and moist against my cheek.

Suddenly my nostrils were filled with the strong odor of fish and seaweed. Overhead the birds' cries grew louder. My eyes snapped open just as the whale broke through the surface of the water!

The giant animal was so close to us, I could see into its open mouth. Its huge lower jaw was lined with sharp, white teeth. It looked to me as if each tooth were as long as a man's forearm—but perhaps that was only my fear.

Up until now, all the whales we hunted had tried to escape from us. But this whale was coming at us as if he were the hunter and we were the victims!

"Jump, lads—save yourselves!" Stubb shouted from the next boat. As we dove over the sides, Moby Dick's enormous jaws began to close around us!

Ahab alone remained in the boat. He stood in the prow, his harpoon raised as if he meant to ram it down the whale's throat. But as the mammoth jaws came closer together, one great white tooth caught in the metal ring of an oarlock.

Cursing, Ahab grabbed the tooth and tried to work it free. But suddenly Moby Dick's tooth slipped out of Ahab's hands. The Captain was thrown into the water just as the powerful jaws crushed the small boat.

The rest of us had already been pulled into other boats. Now we watched helplessly as Moby Dick beat at the water with his great tail, churning it into foam. There was no way we could get to the Captain. It was almost as if the crafty whale *knew* that Ahab was fighting for his life. I saw Ahab struggling to keep his head out of the water, but I feared he would not last much longer.

Then, out of the corner of my eye, I saw the *Pequod* sailing toward us. Threading its way like a needle, the big ship carefully edged between the whale and Captain Ahab, driving the big whale away.

Several of the small whale boats gave chase to the white whale, but the great beast had escaped. I sensed, however, that this was not the last we would see of Moby Dick. And I knew what would happen when the whale returned: The final battle between the Captain and the whale would take place.

9 Remembering Fedallah's Prophecy

The next day the great white whale was sighted again. Again, the three whale boats were quickly lowered. But as we rowed toward the whale, the beast suddenly turned and rushed toward *us*!

Captain Ahab cheered wildly. "I will meet you head on, murderous creature!" he cried out in a mad voice. Then, rising up in the bow of his boat, he steadied himself and raised his harpoon.

Almost at once, the whale swerved, rushing at the other two boats. His mouth gaped open, and his mighty tail beat the water. The harpooners hurled their weapons. But they might as well have tossed pins at the creature. Because of the whale's great speed, the weapons did little harm—they only made him angrier.

Then Moby Dick lowered his head again and turned toward Ahab's boat. With a powerful thrust, the beast cut through the water, ramming the small craft. Fedallah thrust his harpoon deep into Moby Dick's hump. But the whale boat splintered—and again the Captain and his men were thrown into the ocean. And once again the faithful *Pequod* came to the rescue.

When the Captain was pulled on board the ship, we saw that his ivory leg was broken. "Give me a hand, Starbuck," the Captain growled. "I will kill that beast yet— no matter what it takes. Even if I have to chase him around the world ten times!"

But just as Starbuck reached out to take the Captain's arm, Tashtego shouted, "Where's Fedallah?"

We looked around the deck, but Fedallah was not on board. No one had to say another word; we all knew what Fedallah's sad fate had been.

"For the love of God, give up the chase, Captain," Starbuck begged. "Your friend Fedallah has been pulled to the bottom of the sea. Must we *all* die? Give up this madness!"

Suddenly I remembered Fedallah's warning. He had told Ahab that he would die first so that he could pilot Captain Ahab to the next world. How had Fedallah known? Or was it just by chance that Ahab's harpooner had died today? I felt sick.

Ahab pushed aside Starbuck's arm, almost falling overboard as he did so. The Captain glared at his first mate. "I *must* go on, Starbuck," Ahab said. "I vow that tomorrow will be Moby Dick's last day of life!" Then he called for the ship's carpenter to make him a new leg.

Three days went by. On the third morning we saw that it was to be a fair weather day. The sea was calm, the sky clear. But Ahab was in an impatient mood. For a while he stumped back and forth across the deck. We knew he was waiting for the lookout to call out that the whale had been spotted.

When no such signal was heard, Ahab ordered the sailors to raise him up to the top of the main mast. Before long he bellowed out the signal. "There she blows! It is the white whale! Lower the boats."

As the whale boats were lowered into the water, we saw dark fins circling the *Pequod*. *Sharks!* As any sailor knows, they are the vultures of the sea. Surely they were waiting for the hunt to begin and for blood to stain the waves.

The whale boats moved swiftly toward the white hump, their oars cutting cleanly through the water. Ahab's boat led the chase. Now that his harpooner was gone, Ahab carried his own harpoon.

As we neared the white monster, I saw that the whale seemed to be swimming more slowly. He had lost a lot of blood. Perhaps he was tiring of the hunt. I prayed that today would see an end to the madness. Like Starbuck, I wanted to go home.

Now Ahab rose in the prow of his boat, balancing the long harpoon. The boat floated so close to the whale that Ahab might have been able to reach out and touch it. Instead he plunged his weapon into the whale's side. Blood spurted from the new wound. I thought of all the harpoons that were already in the whale. I thought of all the blood the poor, dumb animal had shed and all the pain it had suffered. How cruel and senseless it all seemed!

Ahab dropped back, crouching low in the boat. He watched the whale with a greedy look in his eyes. The wounded creature, crazed with pain and rage, then dove below the waves. As the waters closed over him, there was a horrible silence, like the calm before a storm.

Then suddenly the beast reappeared, erupting out of the water in full fury. For the first time we could see the entire length of the magnificent creature, from his blow hole to his tail. And we could clearly see the tangle of ropes and twisted harpoons caught in his thick hide.

We all drew back in horror when we saw one of the burdens the great whale carried. *Fedallah was caught in the tangled line of his harpoon!* His dead eyes gazed blindly at us. We saw that the little fish of the sea had been nibbling at his dead white flesh. One side of his skull was exposed. One arm, fallen loose from the rope, swung back and forth as if he were calling us to follow him to his watery grave.

"The *prophecy*!" Tashtego cried out. "Fedallah said the Captain would see a hearse not made of human hands."

"Fool! What nonsense are you spouting now?" Stubb shouted. He sounded angry, but frightened, too, as were we all.

"Don't you see? A hearse carries a body to its grave," Flask moaned. "Fedallah is being carried to his grave by a whale. And a whale is not made by human hands."

I shuddered. So far, all that Fedallah had foretold was coming true.

Ahab was now so close that when the whale spouted, the water sprayed over his face. "Aha! Moby Dick, we meet face to face this time," Ahab shouted.

The whale turned, as if he'd heard and understood Ahab's words. In that moment I saw, in that whale's eye, the same light I had seen in Captain Ahab's eyes when he talked about revenge.

Again the whale charged at Ahab's boat.

And again the Captain rose with a harpoon clutched in his fist. As the whale rammed the boat, Ahab threw the harpoon.

Then, in a strange twist of fate, the rope from his harpoon caught Ahab around the neck. As the boat splintered and the men went overboard, the Captain was pulled through the water behind the whale. Then Moby Dick dove straight down, towing Captain Ahab behind him into the depths of the cold green sea. I remembered Fedallah's prophecy—that Ahab's hearse would be a rope. And so it was.

§10 Moby Dick's Revenge

Fortunately, I had been thrown clear of the whale boat before it sank. Now I followed my shipmates as they swam toward the ship.

Then all of a sudden Moby Dick appeared out of nowhere. He began to swim toward the *Pequod*, too! His great body cut through the water like a white knife, his massive tail churning. *Our ship was his target!*

I stopped swimming and treaded water, waiting. As I watched, the whale lowered his great head and rammed the *Pequod* at full tilt. I heard the groan and crackle of wood splintering. Again and again the whale hit the ship, until the masts and spars broke and fell down onto the deck. I heard the screams of men caught under the falling timbers. I watched as wooden planks buckled and tore apart, as nails popped loose, and the glass panes in the cabin windows exploded.

Moby Dick seemed to be crazed. He didn't stop ramming the *Pequod* until a great gash opened up in the side of the ship. Water flooded into the hold. As she took on more and more water, the big ship began to sink. Finally, all that was left was a tangle of spars and sails, oil barrels and wooden chests, canvas and rope, floating on the water.

Now Moby Dick began to swim around and around the wreckage like a great cat playing with a mouse. Suddenly I understood why. As he swam faster and faster, he was summoning up every ounce of strength to create a great whirlpool.

The remains of the ship began to swirl around and around, slowly at first, then faster and faster. I saw what was left of the ship slide toward the center of that whirlpool and then disappear—as if down a huge drain hole. I thought of Fedallah's prophecy about a second hearse made of wood from America. That hearse must be the *Pequod*!

Then the ship was gone. Gone, too, were all who had been aboard her—Starbuck, Flask, Stubb, Tashtego, and Daggoo—and all the other men I'd lived and worked with for so long. Saddest of all, I had in that instant lost my dear friend, Queequeg.

The great white whale floated quietly for a moment, as if examining his work. I wondered if he was pleased with what he'd done. But then I saw the pools of his blood that were staining the water. I knew that neither Captain Ahab nor the whale had been the winner in this battle.

I watched as if in a trance. I saw Moby Dick dive one last time, the water closing over his great white body like a green shroud.

Still treading water, I looked around to see if at least one other crewman might still be alive. But the sea was silent and empty. After a few minutes I was certain that no one else had survived. Now I realized that I was horribly alone in the middle of the vast ocean—with no boat, no food, and no water! I wondered how long I could last.

Then suddenly, I felt something bump

against my shoulder. I gasped in fear, sure that I'd been found by the sharks. To my surprise, it was Queequeg's coffin! The ship's carpenter had done a good job. It was indeed watertight and it made a perfect life preserver.

I managed to pull myself onto the coffin and floated there, too weak to worry about what fate awaited me. The sun sank, then rose again. By late afternoon of the second day, I knew I could not last much longer.

Then, on the horizon, I saw a ship sailing

toward me. At first I thought I must be imagining it. But as the ship came nearer I saw that it was the *Rachel*! Once again, they had been out searching for Captain Gardiner's lost boy. Instead, they had found another orphan of the sea.